FEB 2018

Rabbid of the Sea

adapted by Cordelia Evans

based on the screenplay written by Hervé Benedetti and Nicolas Robin

illustrated by Jim Durk

Ready-to-Read

Simon Spotlight

New York   London   Toronto   Sydney   New Delhi

SIMON SPOTLIGHT
An imprint of Simon & Schuster Children's Publishing Division
1230 Avenue of the Americas, New York, New York 10020
This Simon Spotlight edition May 2015
© 2015 Ubisoft Entertainment. All rights reserved. Rabbids, Ubisoft, and the Ubisoft logo are trademarks of
Ubisoft Entertainment in the U.S. and/or other countries.
All rights reserved, including the right of reproduction in whole or in part in any form.
SIMON SPOTLIGHT, READY-TO-READ, and colophon are registered trademarks of Simon & Schuster, Inc.
For information about special discounts for bulk purchases, please contact Simon & Schuster Special Sales at
1-866-506-1949 or business@simonandschuster.com.
Designed by Maryam Choudhury
Manufactured in the United States of America 0415 LAK
2 4 6 8 10 9 7 5 3 1
ISBN 978-1-4814-3546-8 (hc)
ISBN 978-1-4814-3545-1 (pbk)
ISBN 978-1-4814-3547-5 (eBook)

CONTENTS

CHAPTER 1:
WISH UPON A STARFISH

Four Rabbids were walking along the shore, seeing what sort of trouble they could get themselves into. Well, it's unclear if Rabbids find trouble or trouble finds them, but either way—it happens.

Anyway, trouble came this time in the form of a pink starfish resting calmly in the sand. Resting calmly until one of the Rabbids stepped on it, that is.

The Rabbid didn't know what a starfish was. He just knew it looked like a fun new toy.

At this point, the fact that there was only one starfish and there were four Rabbids became a problem. The other Rabbids wanted to play with the starfish too! Soon the Rabbids began to fight over the starfish.

In most fights there's a winner and loser. And in this case, the loser got smacked in the face with a starfish.

And if one Rabbid gets smacked in the face with a starfish, you know what's going to happen...

All the Rabbids will get smacked in the face with a starfish.

CHAPTER 2:
START OVER

Meanwhile, not far away, an old man was trying to sneak out of his beach shop to go fishing.

"Hey!" called his wife. "Louie! You're not going anywhere until you've washed that window. It needs to shine!"

Louie adjusted his hearing aid so that he couldn't hear his wife's yelling.

"Don't worry, I'll have it all clean in two shakes of a lamb's tail," he said. He got to work washing the store window.

No sooner did Louie step away from the window and say, "Sweetie, it's done!" than a bright pink ball came soaring through the air and landed right on the clean window.

What was the pink ball? You guessed it, it was a starfish rolled up in a ball. A starfish thrown by a Rabbid, of course.

The starfish slid down the glass and fell off the window, leaving a trail of purple slime along the way.

Louie's wife came outside to inspect the window.

"You call that finished?" she shouted. "I call that filthy! Start over."

Louie sighed and picked up his squeegee to wipe away the slime. But the starfish had attached itself to the squeegee, so Louie pulled it off and tossed it toward the shore. If he had known where it was going to land, he probably wouldn't have thrown the starfish in that direction.

But there was no way he could have known it would land . . .

... directly on a Rabbid's head.

Instead of peeling the starfish off his head and throwing it at another Rabbid (like he had before) the Rabbid realized that the starfish on his head looked kind of . . . cool.

Soon three of the Rabbids had found different ways to make the starfish the perfect accessory.

They were so busy cracking themselves up over their new outfits that they didn't wonder where the fourth Rabbid had gone.

Until he cleared his throat, behind them. "Bwah-ah-ah." They turned around to find that this Rabbid was wearing an even better accessory.

An octopus.

The other three Rabbids stared in awe at the Rabbid with the octopus on his head.

"Bwoh," they breathed. An octopus was so much cooler than the starfish they were wearing!

The cool Rabbid demonstrated some of the ways one can wear an octopus. First he shaped the octopus's legs into a mohawk and strutted around like a punk rocker.

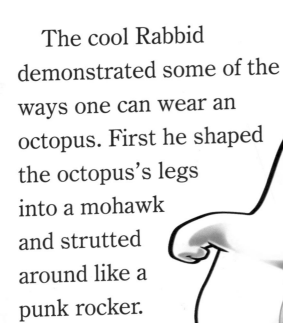

Then he curled the legs onto his forehead and danced like Elvis.

CHAPTER 3:
THE OCTOPUS STRIKES BACK

Well, the three Rabbids were so impressed by the cool Rabbid that they decided the starfish they were wearing were no longer cool at all. They pulled the starfish off their bodies and tossed them away.

And you can probably guess where they landed.

If you guessed they landed on the store window that Louie had just washed for the second time, you'd be exactly right.

But unfortunately, Louie didn't notice that before he called his wife to inspect his cleaning job.

"What?" said his wife when she came outside to find the three starfish sliding slimily down the window. "Are you kidding me? Now it's even worse than it was before!"

Louie's face fell as he followed her gaze to the starfish.

Back at the shore, the Rabbids were still entranced by the octopus. The octopus, however, was not feeling quite as entranced by the Rabbids. And unlike the starfish, the octopus had a way to fight back. In fact, it had eight ways.

First the octopus used its legs to poke the Rabbid in the shoulder, which made the Rabbid turn around in circles to see who was poking him.

Then the octopus used its legs to cover the Rabbid's eyes, so he was wobbling around crazily, unable to see where he was going.

The other three Rabbids laughed hysterically at the fourth Rabbid. They loved to watch the octopus annoy him!

But the octopus was fed up with the laughing Rabbids, too. When the Rabbid it was riding got close enough to the other three, the octopus used some of its legs to send those Rabbids flying!

CHAPTER 4:
RABBIDS VS. THE OCTOPUS

The Rabbids had been perfectly happy to let the octopus torture their fellow Rabbid with its legs, but now that it had taken out some of its anger on them, they weren't very happy anymore.

One of the Rabbids walked toward the octopus with an intimidating glare.

The Rabbid tugged on the octopus, trying to pull it off the other Rabbid's head, but the octopus batted the Rabbid away with one of its legs. So the Rabbid tried again, and was *again* batted away by the octopus.

Try as he might, the Rabbid could not knock the octopus off the other Rabbid's head. Not only that, the octopus knocked the Rabbid off his feet—again!

The Rabbids were so annoyed they were about to cause a lot of trouble. Well, let's be honest, they always cause a lot of trouble, but they cause even more trouble when they're annoyed!

Each Rabbid grabbed one of the octopus's legs and pulled as hard as he possibly could. The octopus tried its best to hold onto the fourth Rabbid's head, but with three Rabbids tugging and pulling on it, it lost its grip . . .

. . . and went soaring through the air toward
Louie's store.

CHAPTER 5:
KUNG-FU LOUIE

Now, I know what you're thinking. You're thinking the octopus landed right smack on the store window that Louie had just cleaned for the *third* time. But give Louie a little more credit! He wasn't about to get yelled at by his wife for a *third* time, too!

This time, he saw the octopus flying toward his sparkling window. And, with surprising agility for a man his age, he caught the octopus, and redirected it away from his clean window.

Louie was very happy and proud of himself. Unfortunately, he wasn't going to be happy for long, because of where the octopus had landed.

No, it didn't land back by the Rabbids this time.

Louie had redirected the octopus toward the highway, where it just so happened that an escaped convict had been speeding down the road with three police cars in hot pursuit.

Now do you know where the octopus
landed? Yup—right on the windshield of
the convict's car. (Well, it wasn't actually
his car. It was stolen. But he was driving it
when the octopus hit it.)

The car swerved out of control, and rounded the corner in front of Louie's store, just as Louie was telling his wife the window was finally clean and strolling away with his fishing rod. But she didn't even have time to get up from her chair, because, as you've probably guessed . . .

. . . the swerving car crashed right into
the store window, shattering the glass
completely.

CHAPTER 6:
THE LATEST TREND

In all the chaos that ensued, the flying octopus once again landed on someone's head: Louie's wife.

"Louie!" she screeched, waving her arms blindly in front of her. But Louie was already far down the beach (remember, the surprising agility) and hadn't heard the crash—or his wife screeching. Unless he had turned his hearing aid back on, but we'll never know if that was the case.

The escaped convict crawled dizzily out
of the car and was immediately surrounded
by the police cars, which, not having octopi
on their windshields, hadn't crashed.

The convict was taken into custody. So at
least one good thing came of the Rabbids'
mischief!

Meanwhile, down at the shore, the Rabbids were completely unaware of the crash—and arrest—they'd caused. They were more focused on another new fashion trend they'd discovered: when they'd pulled the octopus off the Rabbid, bright pink spots remained on their skin.

Obviously all the Rabbids wanted bright pink spots now. Luckily, a toy plunger blaster had landed on the shore amongst the debris from the crash. The Rabbids got to work shooting plungers at each other to achieve their desired look.

And Louie got to work fishing. But, as we've learned, sitting that close to a group of Rabbids is quite dangerous, so it's likely he didn't fish in peace very long.